This book belongs to

....

Written by Amy Boxshall.
Illustrated by Stephanie Thannhauser.

Squasherella

Amy Boxshall • Stephanie Thannhauser

make
believe
ideas

Squasherella — Squash for short —
was **kind** and **sweet** and **cute**,
but longed to be like all the other
scary veg and **fruit**.

BOo!

Her sisters could make any veg
jump out of their skin!
But all that Squash could manage
was a big and friendly grin.

At Scare School, all the fruit and veg played **tricks** on Squash each day.

She couldn't shine at Glow Class,

nor frighten veg away.

Boo!

So when Squash was invited
to the big Halloween Ball,
her sisters told her,

"You **can't** go, you're not

scary at all!"

Dear *Squasherella,*

You are invited to the
HALLOWEEN BALL
to find out who is the
SCARIEST of them all!

All entries will be welcomed,
but only one will be crowned
the SPOOKIEST.

Yours sincerely,
Miss W. Itch
Head Party Planner

Squash was sad but thought, "It's true.
I don't think I look right.

I'll never be a scary fruit
whose face can spook and fright."

Feeling glum, Squash stayed at home.
But – in a **flash** – she found
a magic Fairy Squash-mother
had popped out of the ground!

"I'll help you to look scary," the nice Squash-mother cried.

"But remember that true scariness must come from the inside."

One wave of the magic wand gave Squash a **spooky grin**,

an **eerie glow,**

twiggy vines

and a **car** to travel in.

As Squasherella reached the **ball**,
a **voice** rang in her head:

"The **magic** ends at **midnight**,"

Fairy Squash-mother had said.

At the door, the bouncer called,
"Now, POSE and shout out

BOO!

The WINNER is the SCARIEST —
perhaps it will be YOU!"

The other guests all turned and gasped
as Squash came through the door.
She rushed to see her sisters,
feeling **braver** than before.

At once, she made a SCARY face.
Her sisters jumped in fear.
"Who are **you**?" they shouted.
"You're the
scariest
fruit here!"

Squash was having so much fun,
she soon lost track of time.
And suddenly, the great big clock

began to chime ...

chime ...

chime.

Squash's **crown** dropped from her head
as she began to flee.
"I've got to **leave** right now,"
she thought,
"or they'll see the **real me!**"

The sisters spied the flower crown
and **cried** out to the ball,

"It was **Squash**
who
scared us…

SPOOKY WALL OF FAME

she's the **scariest** of all!"

She decided to **spook**
all the veg.
She crept to them,
then **moaned** ...

BOOOOOOOOOOO!

The fruit and veg leapt up in shock.
They **loved** to get a **fright**!

"**Squash**, you are the **scariest** of everyone tonight!

Even though you may look **cute** and have a **button nose**, you still managed to **scare** us from our **top leaves** to our **toes**."

Most of all Squash understood:
"There's **nothing** I can't be.

Anything can happen
if I believe in me."

The End